The Elevator Family Plays Hardball

You might enjoy these other titles by Douglas Evans:

The Elevator Family	*Delacorte Press*
The Elevator Family Takes a Hike	*WT Melon*
The Classroom at the End of the Hall	*Front Street*
Math Rash and Other Classroom Tales	*Front Street*
Mouth Moths, More Classroom Tales	*Front Street*
Apple Island, or the Truth About Teachers	*Front Street*
MVP: Magellan Voyage Project	*Front Street*

The Elevator Family Plays Hardball

Douglas Evans

Rousing sequel to The Elevator Family

WT Melon
www.wtmelon.com
"good stories; good tunes"

ISBN: 1517601312
ISBN-13: 978-1517601317

For Jane

B*rrrrrrrring!*

Walter Wilson sat up in his sleeping bag. The room was inky dark.

"Great Scott!" he said. "What was that bell?"

Winona Wilson, lying beside her husband, rolled onto her side. "The school bell, dear," she said. "Remember what day this is?"

Walter's face brightened. "Of course. Whitney and Winslow's first day of school."

"Happy Valley Elementary School," said Winona. "What a pleasant name. How lucky we were to find these excellent accommodations right outside the twin's new classroom."

"Only the best!" said Walter. "Only the best will do for the Wilson family."

He reached up and pulled a light switch chord. A single bare light bulb lit up a long, narrow room. A row of brass hooks stuck out of the side wall and above the hooks ran a long shelf. At the end of the room was a wooden door and on the door hung an embroidered sampler with the words HOME SWEAT HOME stitched into it.

"Morning, children," Walter and Winona said together.

Before the door stood the ten-year-old Wilson twins, Winslow and Whitney, already dressed for school.

"We better be going," said Whitney. "We don't want to be late on our first day."

"I'm a bit nervous," said Winslow. "I hope the other kids like us. I hope we have a good teacher."

"Nothing wrong with first-day jitters," said Walter. "It calms the butteries in your belly."

"You'll make new friends in no time, dear," said Winona. "You fit in wherever we go."

Whitney opened the door, letting in the chatter and laughter of many children. With a wave to their parents, the twins stepped from the long room.

"Our children have grown up so quickly," Winona said. "Two shakes of a lamb's tail. A wink of an eye."

Walter yawned. "Right now I'd like to catch forty more winks," he said.

Brrrrrriiiing! The bell sounded again outside the narrow room.

Walter winced. "Great Scott! Maybe not."

"Walter, let's get up and start our day, too," Winona said. "Happy Valley seems like such a friendly town to explore."

"And maybe we can find a new place to stay tonight," said Walter. "Just as cozy and convenient, but quieter. My ears are still ringing."

The two Wilsons rose and got dressed. They rolled up the sleeping bags and packed them in their wheeled luggage bags.

While they worked, the door opened. A boy and girl wearing backpacks stood in the doorway. Their eyes went wide.

"Who are you?" asked the boy.

"What are you doing in here?" asked the girl?

"We're Walter and Winona Wilson," said Walter. "We just moved to Happy Valley."

"We're the proud parents of Whitney and Winslow, your new classmates," said Winona.

"Oh," said the boy.

"Cool," said the girl.

Both students quickly hung their backpacks on a hook and left the room.

"Such nice children," said Winona.

"Bright and inquisitive," said Walter

He removed the HOME SWEAT HOME sampler from the door and packed it in his bag.

"Home Sweat Home hangs wherever the Wilsons stay," he said.

"And I have a feeling Happy Valley will be a place where we'll stay for a long time," said Winona.

Pulling their wheeled luggage behind them, Walter and Winona left the long room. They found themselves in the back of a classroom with four rows of desks facing a large teacher's desk. Behind the desk sat the teacher, a tall woman with brown hair tied in a bun. On the desk stood a small French flag and a brass statue of the Eiffel Tower.

The teacher smiled at the two Wilsons. "May I help you?" she said.

Winona pointed to Whitney and Winslow sitting in the front row. "They're ours," she said.

"Educate them well," said Walter.

"You must be Mr. and Mrs. Wilson," said the teacher. "I'm Miss Potts. The class is thrilled to have new members."

"Excellent accommodations you have here, madam," said Walter.

The teacher's eyebrows rose. "But that...but this is." She couldn't get the words out.

"Sorry we can't stay longer," said Winona. "But we have so much to do today."

Then, giving the thumbs-up sign to the twins, the two Wilsons strolled from the room.

Walter and Winona walked down the school hallway. They waved to Mr. Smear, the school custodian, who stood in his small custodian's room, washing a mop.

"Morning, sir," Winona said. "Lovely place you have there."

"Fits me fine," said the janitor.

Farther down the hall, the Wilsons stopped to admire the tiny teacher's supply room with its tidy shelves of paper and paint bottles.

"Excellent," said Walter.

"Wonderful," said Winona. "No wasted space."

Finally, they waved to Miss Natalie, the school secretary, who sat in the compact school office.

"Thanks for the refreshing stay," said Winona.

"You might want to tone down that bell a bit, though," said Walter.

The Wilsons left the school by way of the playground door.

"Bracing morning," Walter said, sucking in a lungful of air. "All is right with the world."

The couple strolled onto the playground that offered the usual monkey bars, four-square courts, hopscotch patterns, and tire swings. In an area filled with sawdust rose a tall climbing structure with shiny blue and orange climbing bars.

Under the structure sat Cat, the Wilson's scruffy gray dog. When he spotted Walter and Winona, he bounded toward them, ears flapping and tail wagging.

"Top of the morning, old pal," Walter said, giving the dog a hearty pat on the back. "Hope you slept well."

Winona looked toward the top of the climbing structure.

"Look there, Walter," she said. "That little cabin appears to be vacant."

She pointed to a small cabin no bigger than a garden shed. Its sides and roof were of plastic molded to look like logs. A sign above the open doorway read: Fort Wilderness.

"Unfortunately Fort Wilderness is too close to the school bell," Walter said. "I'd be disturbed while writing my book."

Winona gave Walter a look. "Your what?"

"I plan to write a book, Winona," Walter said. "A collection of our family's adventures. I will call it *The Ups and Down of the Elevator Family."*

Winona picked up a tennis ball and tossed it into a large grass field. Cat took off after it, scattering four robins that were searching for worms.

"Good for you," Winona said. "If you are going to write about our family I can do some sketches for it."

Cat trotted back with the ball in his mouth. He dropped it at Winona's feet. She tossed it farther into the field, and the dog sprinted off again.

Walter punched a tetherball and watched it twirl around and around the pole. "Excellent idea," he said. "And I spy a perfect place to begin my writing."

Behind the playground asphalt, was a dirt baseball diamond with plastic bases and a tall wire backstop. Next to the first base line stood a long wooden building.

The Wilsons stepped up to the building. Half of it was below ground. Three steps led down to rubber mats that covered the floor. The place had many shelves, a table at each end, and a long wooden bench running its entire length.

"How quaint," said Winona. "It's far enough from the bell, but still close enough to the school, so the twins won't have to walk far."

"It even has a power plug for my laptop," said Walter. "I'll feel like a real writer in this basement studio apartment."

Winona shook her head. "But whoever stayed in this apartment last left sunflower seeds all over the floor. Messy, messy, messy."

A large sign painted on the back wall of the studio read:

GO COOTS!

"What a curious sign," said Winona. "What's a coot and where do they want it to go."

Walter took his iPhone from a pocket and checked the Internet. "Coot: a black duck-like bird with big feet and a fat bill," said Walter. "It's also called a mud hen. But it says nothing among them going anywhere."

"Perhaps that's the name of this apartment," Winona suggested. "The Coots Apartment."

"Excellent! All in favor of staying in the Coots Apartment say *aye*," said Walter.

"Aye," said Winona.

Walter and Winona rolled their luggage down the steps. They unpacked the sleeping bags and laid them head to toe on the long shelf. While Winona swept up the sunflower seeds, Walter hung the HOME SWEAT HOME sampler next to the GO COOTS! sign. Then he placed his laptop upon an end table and plugged it in.

"All set to begin writing," he said.

Having retrieved the tennis ball, Cat came racing back with it in his mouth. Winona tossed it back to the field and took out her sketchpad and pencil.

"And I'm ready to begin drawing," she said.

Walter sat on the bench and opened the laptop lid. He wiggled his fingers and said, "A forty-thousand-word book begins with a single letter."

Then he typed:

The Ups and Downs of the Elevator Family

by Walter Wilson

For the next two hours, Walter tapped on his laptop, while Winona drew pictures in her sketchpad. In the meantime, Cat ran between the long apartment and field retrieving the tennis ball Winona threw out for him.

"That pooch never runs out of energy," Walter said.

"And Cat's a remarkable ball catcher," said Winona. "How's the book going, Walter?"

"Only the best. The first chapter is about the birth of the twins in a compact ambulance on the way to the hospital."

Winona smiled. "Back when we were living in the small cabin far out on the ice on Lake Winnibigoshish."

At ten o'clock the school bell rang.

Winona lowered her sketchpad. "Not too loud and not too soft," she said.

"As Goldilocks once said, just right," said Walter.

As he spoke, a school door flew open and children streamed onto the playground. They fanned out across the asphalt, bouncing red balls and kicking yellow ones.

"How exciting," said Winona. "There are Whitney and Winslow." She waved, and the twins over to the long apartment.

"How do you like the new place?" Walter asked.

"Fantabulous," said Winslow, admiring the building from the top step.

"Much more sunshine and fresh air than the place we stayed in last night," said Whitney.

"We can watch all the playground action right from here," said Winona.

"Watch me on the monkey bars," said Whitney.

"And I'm going to play four-square," said

Winslow.

After the twins left, Miss Potts, who was on recess duty, walked over. She wore a blue beret, a red coat, and a white scarf. A pin on her coat said I ♥ Paris. She held a silver whistle.

"*Ruff! Ruff!*" went Cat.

"Greetings, Miss Potts," said Winona. "Nice of you to come for a visit"

Walter paused with his fingers on the laptop keyboard. "How are the twins doing?" he asked.

"They are excellent students," said the teacher. "Top in the class in reading and math."

"Only the best," said Walter.

"Where did they attend school previously," the teacher asked. "Where did they learn so much?"

"Homeschooled mostly," said Winona.

"Road schooled, actually," said Walter. "We travel a lot and the road has been their education."

"We enrolled them in your school so they can meet other children," said Winona.

Miss Potts turned toward the playground and

blew her whistle. “One down on the slide at a time,” she shouted.

Walter studied the woman’s beret and pin. “Have just returned from France, madam?” he said.

The teacher shook her head. “No, I’ve never been there. But I’m very fond of French food, French literature, French movies, anything French.”

“Last year we stayed in a marvelous cabin right along the Champs-Élysées in Paris,” said Winona. “It was filled with newspapers and magazines.”

“Ooo la laaa,” said Walter.

“I can only dream of going to France,” said Miss Potts. “I never have time for travel. I’ve never found the right traveling companion.”

“The Wilsons are good at making time,” said Walter.

“And fortunately we’re our favorite companions.”

Again the teacher blew her whistle. “Stop kicking the red balls!” she called out. To the Wilsons, she said, “Yes, making time is what I must do. But right now it’s time for me to return to my recess duty.”

After the teacher left, Walter and Winona looked for Winslow and Whitney on the playground. To their surprise, they stood alone by the school door.

"Oh, dear, the twins look so glum," said Winona.

"How odd!" said Walter. "They've enjoyed every playground we've ever played on."

"But no one seems to want to play with them," said Winona. "What could be the problem?"

Brrrrrrrring!

"Recess is over," Miss Potts announced from her position at the center of the asphalt. "Everyone back to class!"

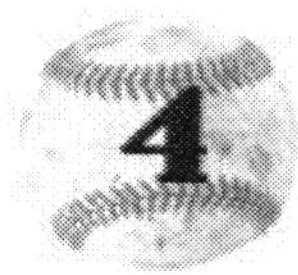

4

At twelve o'clock the school bell rang again. Students streamed out to the playground, swinging lunch bags and boxes. Winslow and Whitney ran to the Coots Apartment with two classmates, Benson Field and Nora Lee.

"Guests are always welcome where the Wilsons stay," said Walter

"I've prepared Waldorf salad for lunch," said Winona. "There's plenty for everyone."

"This is where you're staying?" Benson asked. "Cool!"

"We just moved in," said Walter."

"Isn't it fantabulous?" said Winslow.

"We're a tight-knit family," said Whitney.

Winona covered a table with a checkered tablecloth and placed a large salad bowl, paper plates, and plastic forks upon it.

"Please begin," she said to her guests.

Nora scooped salad onto a plate. "This lunch sure beats the Chef's Surprise they're serving in the cafeteria," she said.

"And the Chef's Special they served yesterday," said Benson.

The Wilson's and their two guests ate lunch on the apartment steps. Cat sat outside, eyeing the salad plates.

Walter pointed to the **Go Coots!** sign on the wall. "Do either of you know the meaning of this?" he asked the visitors.

"The Coots are the name of our Little League team," Nora explained. "Our first practice is this evening on this baseball field."

"My dad is the coach," said Benson.

"I'm the Coot's pitcher," said Nora. She smiled at

the twins. "Why don't you join our team? We need players."

The twins grabbed Walter's arm. "Can we?" they asked together

"If your mother agrees," said Walter.

"As long as you have your homework is done before practice," said Winona. "We'll sign you up this afternoon."

"How was school?" Walter asked.

"Your teacher said you were high in your class," said Winona. "But we noticed you weren't having much fun during recess."

"Kids refused to play with us," said Whitney.

"Everyone ignored us," said Winslow.

"That's because of Irene Towne," said Nora. "She's a fifth-grade who rules the playground."

"Irene, the Tetherball Queen," said Benson. "She's terrific a tetherball player, but she's also a bully."

"Irene told everyone not to play with the new kids," said Nora.

"Irene Towne controls everything on the

playground," said Benson. "Who gets to play what game, who gets to use what ball. Everything."

"That doesn't make Happy Valley very happy," said Winona. "Why don't you tell the teachers about Irene."

"We do," said Nora. "Mrs. Franklin, our principal, talks to Irene, and then she leaves us alone for a few days. But after that, she goes back to being her bully self."

"Irene's mom is president of the PTA," said Benson. "So Mrs. Franklin doesn't want to upset Irene too much."

Winslow held up his fork. "There's only one way to handle a bully like Irene Towne," he said. "Beat her at her own game."

Nora and Benson's eyes went wide.

"You mean, you're going to challenge Irene in tetherball?" Benson asked.

"No one has ever beaten Irene before," said Nora.

"But if I *could* beat her at tetherball, she'd be taken down a notch," said Winslow. "Kids would see she isn't so powerful after all."

"Excellent idea," said Walter. "No more Irene, the Tetherball Queen."

"And the Coots Apartment is very close to the tetherball court," said Winona. "You would have lots of time to practice."

Walter pulled on his suspenders. "And I can give you a few tetherball tips," he said. "I was quite the tetherball champ in my school days. Only the best."

After school, while the twins did their homework, Walter poured charcoal onto his barbecue grill. With Little League practice starting that evening, the Wilsons were having a picnic dinner.

"I'll grill bratwurst sausages," Walter said. "Nothing like bratwurst at a baseball game."

He sprinkled on an ample amount of lighter fluid, threw on a match, and *Phoom!* instant barbecue.

"*Take me out to the ball game*," he sang while the bratwurst cooked.

Cat howled along with the tune.

Around 5 PM, Whitney and Winslow changed into their new uniforms, white baseball pants and black jerseys with the word Coots in white script written across the front. Whitney had a big white 3 on the back and Winslow had a 7. Their black caps had a white bill like that of a coot bird.

Nora Lee arrived with her parents. While she tossed a ball back and forth with the twins, Mr. and Mrs. Lee joined Walter and Winona at the barbecue grill.

“Care for a bratwurst?” Walter said.

“Don’t mind if I do,” said Mr. Lee.

“Nice idea,” said Mrs. Lee. “A picnic at practice.”

“We met Nora at lunchtime,” said Winona.

Walter looked out toward the pitcher's mound. “And she has a topnotch throwing arm.”

“Yes, we expect top quality from everything our daughter does,” said Mrs. Lee. “She must get top grades, must be top in her ballet class, must be a top piano player, and must get her into a top college.”

“Winslow and Whitney can’t top that,” said Walter, handing both Lees a bratwurst in a bun.

“But Winslow is great at pick-up sticks and

Whitney's an expert on the monkey bars," said Winona.

Benson Field showed up with his father, Sadler Field, the Coots' manager. Without a word, Benson wandered out to right field. He stood there with his mitt by his side, staring up at the sky.

"You must be Mr. and Mrs. Wilson," Mr. Field said to Walter and Winona. "Good to have Whitney and Winslow on the team. That brings us up to eight players. We are still short one player, but this will have to do."

Winona looked to right field. "What's wrong with Benson?" she asked. "He looks lost in his thoughts."

The coach nodded. "Benson daydreams a lot," he said. "Ever since his mother passed away last year, his mind has been wandering more and more. He spends most of his time alone. I thought if he joins this baseball team, he'd be more focused and happier."

"Care for a bratwurst?" said Walter.

Mr. Field shook his head. "Thanks, but I need to start practice." He cupped his hands to his mouth and called out, "OK, Coots, let's do some fielding."

"Hurrah!" Winona shouted from the cabin steps.

"Go Coots!" called Walter.

"*Ruff! Ruff!*" went Cat.

The Coot players took the field. Whitney played third base and Winslow played first. With only eight players, center field was empty.

Sadler Field, in the batter's box, hit a ground ball to Lilly Spring at second base. It went through Lilly's legs. But Cat leaped from the Coots Apartment and took off after it. He came trotting back with the ball in his mouth and dropped it by Mr. Field.

"Hurrah, Cat!" shouted Winona.

"What a dog!" said Walter.

"Uncanny," said the coach. "That dog grabbed the ball faster than any player I've seen."

Next Sadler Field hit a pop fly to right field. Benson was too busy daydreaming to even notice the ball coming his way. Cat, however, ran out and caught the ball in his mouth.

"Great catch, Cat!" said Walter.

"Good try, Benson," said Winslow

"Uncanny," said Mr. Field. "That dog sure can play baseball."

While the practice continued, parents sat in lounge chairs next to the long apartment.

"Bratwursts! Get your bratwursts here!" Walter shouted as though he were a baseball stadium vendor.

The practice went on for an hour. The Coots players practiced batting, throwing and catching. Cat continued to retrieve the ball that the others missed.

"Uncanny," Sadler Field said over and over.

After practice, Mr. and Mrs. Lee walked away with Nora saying, "And now it's time for your ballet lesson and then you need to practice your piano. You must keep at the top of all your classes."

The rest of the team had orange slices for a snack.

"Excellent first practice, Coach," said Walter. "Only the best."

"Your twins really helped out," Mr. Field said. "Our first game is on Saturday against the Mayfield Gophers. I sure wish Benson would put his heart into the game. His mind wanders when he's out in right field. I wish I knew where it was wandering to."

"He's an excellent, boy," said Walter. "I just hope a fly ball doesn't bonk him on the head before Cat can get to it.

"Ruff! Ruff!" went Cat.

The coach patted the dog on the snout. "I've never seen a dog play ball like Cat," he said.
"This dog is uncanny."

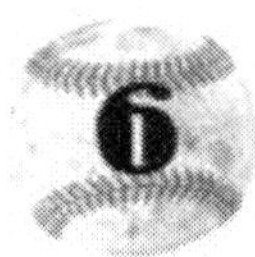

By the time the players left, the sun had set, casting a purple tone across the playground. Walter brought a camping light from the trunk of the Wilson's compact car and hung it from the ceiling of the Coots Apartment. While Walter worked on his book, Winona sketched. The twins sat in Fort Wilderness reading paperbacks by flashlights.

"Chapter Three," Walter said. "The Wilsons check into the Otis Room at the San Francisco Hotel."

"That's where we got the name *The Elevator Family,*" said Winona. She looked out at the playground. "Such a lovely time of the evening. People call it *dusk,* but I think of it as the *Purple Time.*"

A loud clang interrupted the evening silence. Walter and Winona looked toward the school. The tall dark figure of a man stood before the green Dumpster at the side of the building. Next to him stood a shopping cart half-filled with bottles and cans. The man leaned into the Dumpster and came out holding a soda can that he added to the cart.

"A can and bottle collector," said Walter.

"We can give him the cans from the baseball game picnic," said Winona.

Walter climbed to the top of the apartment steps. "Evening, sir," he called out. "Care to join us?"

The man pushed his cart across the baseball diamond. "I thought I saw a light over here," he said. "Didn't want to disturb anyone."

"Guests are always welcome where the Wilsons stay," said Walter. "I'm Walter and this is Winona." The twins came running over. "And here come Whitney and Winslow. They just started school today.

"We were lucky to find this place vacant," said Winona.

The man nodded. "Sometimes I sleep in here myself," he said. "My name is Daniel. Dan, the Can Man the kids call me.

"Have a seat, Dan, and tell us about the can collecting business," said Walter.

The man sat on the top step of the long apartment. He smiled at Walter's laptop. "Are you are a writer?" he asked.

Walter pulled on his suspenders. "I'm writing about my family's adventures."

"Sounds good," said Dan. "Writing is a lot like can collecting, an independent business. No bosses. No one telling you what to do. By cashing in cans and bottles for their deposit money, I make just enough to get by each day. Just enough for a good meal and shelter."

"So you have plenty of time to relax and think," said Winslow.

"And read," said Whitney.

"That I do," Dan, the Can Man said. "Let me tell you a story that demonstrates my way of thinking."

"We love stories," said Winona.

Dan's story went like this:

Once a rich man spotted a fisherman relaxing in a rowboat that was full of fish. The rich man asked the fisherman why he wasn't out catching more fish. The fisherman replied that he had enough fish to get him through the day and tomorrow he would go out and catch some more. The rich man shook his head and told him that if he went out now he could make more money to buy two rowboats. Then he could go out and catch more fish, and with that money, he could buy a whole fleet of rowboats with which he could catch many more fish.

The fisherman laughed and asked what would he do with all that money.

The rich man said, "Um, well, you could retire and relax.'"

When the story was over, the four Wilsons clapped.

"Dan, you seem content," said Walter.

The man stood. "That I am. But now I must be going to collect more cans. If I don't get my daily quota

I don't eat."

Winslow held out a bag of cans from the cookout. "Here , Dan," he said. "I hope these help."

Dan tossed the cans into his shopping cart. "That they will," he said. "Good night now."

After Dan, the Can Man left, the Wilsons sat in lawn chairs outside the Coots Apartment. Winona had bought a string of tiny white lights and strung along the top of the Coots Apartment. The lights now twinkled with the stars that were appearing in the purple sky.

"I love the *purple* time," Winona said.

"Hear the chirps of the crickets and the putt putt of the lawn sprinklers," said Walter. "And not a single bell going off."

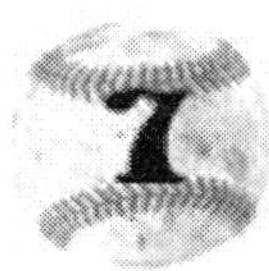

The twins rose before dawn the next morning. They dressed in running shorts, T-shirts, and sneakers and ran to the playground to practice tetherball.

"Irene Towne is about a foot taller than you," Whitney told her brother. "You're going to reach up on your tiptoes."

"I will need to do more than that to beat Irene, the Tetherball Queen," Winslow said. "I need a strategy."

"Tetherball is all about timing and rhythm," Walter called from the Coots Apartment. "Timing and rhythm are everything in tetherball."

After an hour of practice, the twins dressed for

school, ate bowls of Corn Flakes, kissed their parents goodbye, patted Cat on the snout, and took off for school.

"Have a good day," Winona called out.

“Learn well,” said Walter. “See you at recess time

At 8:30 the morning bell rang and the students charged toward the school doors. At 10:00 the bell rang again, and the students charged out the doors. Miss Potts, wearing her blue beret, stood in the middle of the asphalt. Today she wore a scarf printed like the French flag.

“Ooo la laaa,” said Walter.

The twins ran over to the Coots Apartment.

“Today we’re going to stand by the tetherball circle,” said Whitney.

“Oh, dear,” said Winona. “Do you think you’re ready to challenge Irene already?”

“We’re just going to study Irene’s style,” said Winslow. “We’ll look for her weak spots.”

“Excellent,” said Walter. “Watch her timing. Tetherball is all about timing.” He looked toward the tetherball circle. The Tetherball Queen had just whacked the yellow ball and was watching it go around and around the pole, high over a tall fifth-grader's head. "My, is she good."

After recess, a green van pulled into the school parking lot. The van had flower bouquets painted on the side along with the words:
Cathy's Blooms

"*Ruff! Ruff*!" went Cat.

The next thing the Wilsons knew, Cathy, an old friend from San Francisco, stood outside the Coots Apartment. She held a bouquet of carnations. A baby was strapped on her front.

"Cathy!" Walter and Winona shouted as one.

"What a surprise!" said Winona.

"The last time we saw you was at your wedding to Gavin," said Walter.

The girl handed the flowers to Winona. "Hello, Mr. and Mrs. Wilson," she said. "Word has spread throughout Happy Valley that the famous Elevator Family is staying here. The flowers are for your housewarming.

"How kind," said Winona. "This reminds me of the flowers Gavin brought to us in the Otis room during our stay at the San Francisco Hotel, because he was too shy to talk to you in your flower stall."

"And guess what?" said Cathy. "Now I own my own flower delivery business, *Cathy's Blooms*, and I have my own flower delivery van."

"Good for you!" said Walter.

Winona smiled at the baby. "And this must be Rose," she said.

"She's three months old," said Cathy.

"*Ruff! Ruff*!" went Cat.

The baby looked down at the scruffy dog and giggled.

"I think Rose has made a new friend," said Walter.

"How's Gavin?" asked Winona.

"He's almost finished Teacher College," said Cathy. "And guess what? He'll be doing his student teaching this spring at a school right near here."

"Excellent," said Walter. "That means we'll be seeing a lot more of him."

"Unfortunately, I don't see much of my husband," said Cathy. "With a baby and both of us working, we never have time to spend much alone time alone."

"Then you must let us babysit Rose for you," said Winona.

Cathy's eyes brightened. "Oh, would you mind?" she said. "A free evening would be wonderful."

"Certainly," said Walter. "Bring little Rose around the Coots Apartment any time you like. We're usually at home."

"How are Whitney and Winslow?" Cathy asked.

"They started school yesterday," said Walter. "They fit right in."

"In two weeks is their first Little League game," said Winona. "Won't you, Gavin, and Rose join us here."

"We're having a barbecue, and I'm cooking bratwurst," said Walter.

"That sounds delightful," said Cathy. "We'll be here for sure. Now I must be off. Spring is a busy season for flowers."

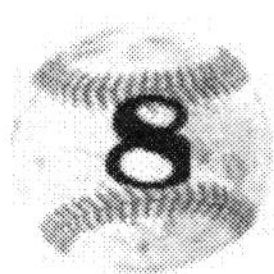

After school, a dozen students walked onto the field holding model rockets.

“Fantabulous,” said Winslow.

“Looks like some sort of club,” said Whitney.

As the four Wilsons watched the rocketeers, a buzzing came from overhead. They looked up to see a small aircraft with four rotating blades hovering over the Coots Apartment. The quadcopter lowered in front of them, and they heard a voice say, “Hello, Wilsons!”

“Great Scott!” said Walter. “That flying thing can talk.”

“It’s me, Benson,” the voice said. “I’m out in the field. You’re talking to my remote control drone.”

The four Wilsons looked out and saw Benson Field standing by one of the rockets. He held a small box with an antenna sticking out the top. The family waved to him and he waved back.

"Benson," said Winslow. "What's happening out there?"

"It's a meeting of the Happy Valley Maker's Club," Benson replied.

"Maker's Club?" said Walter. "And what do you make?"

"We build drones, robots, and stuff. This afternoon we're shooting off rockets. Winslow and Whitney come join us."

As Benson spoke, the first rocket launched. *Swoosh*! It shot straight into the air leaving a smoky tail behind it. Far overhead the rocket stopped climbing. With the aid of an orange parachute, it floated back to the baseball field.

"Fantabulous!" said Winslow.

"Can we go?" said Whitney.

"Certainly," said Walter. "Go make some fun.

"How I love our Coots Apartment," said Winona. "It offers endless entertainment right out the front door."

The twin ran into the field. They approached a man who seemed to be the club leader. He wore a gray T-shirt with NASA written across the front. On his back was a large backpack full of bricks.

"We're Winslow and Whitney Wilsons," said Winslow. "And we wish to join your Maker's Club and make things."

"We're staying in the Coots Apartment by first base," said Whitney.

The man looked toward the long cabin. Walter and Winona waved to him.

"Everyone is welcome in the Maker's Club," the man said. "I'm Kelly. Today is rocket day and next week is 3-D printer day."

Shuuuush! Another rocket took off.

"*Ruff! Ruff!*" went Cat, and he bounded onto the field.

"Why are you wearing that heavy backpack?"

Whitney asked Kelly.

"I'm in training for a long-distance hike," the man said. "Next month I'm thru-hiking the Pacific Crest Trail."

"Fantabulous!" said Winslow. "That's the trail that goes from the Mexican border to the Canadian border."

"It's 2650 miles long," said Whitney. "And you get to sleep in a tiny tent for five whole months."

Kelly nodded and adjusted the weight on his shoulders. "That's why I need to be in great shape," he said.

The twins ran over to Benson who was about to launch the largest rocket in the group, a three-foot-tall model held up with four fins on the bottom."

"I built this rocket myself using parts I found in Dumpsters," Benson said.

"That's awesome, Benson," said Whitney.

"I also mixed my own rocket fuel."

"Really awesome," said Winslow.

"Now I'm ready for the countdown," said Benson,

making a final adjustment to the rocket.

Together they counted down. "Ten, nine, eight, seven, six, five, four, three, two, one...*Blast off*!"

Benson pushed a button, and from beneath the rocket came a flash of light. *Swoosh!* The model soared upward. All heads craned back to watch the rocket fly skyward. High overhead a big parachute popped out of its nose and brought the craft safely back to the ground.

"Benson, you've done it again," Kelly called out.

"Your best rocket yet," said one of the Maker Club members.

In the meantime, Mr. Field arrived on the playground.

"Benson just launched a riveting rocket," Winona called to him.

"The boy's a rocket wizard," said Walter.

"Yes, Benson spends hours going through our neighbor's trash bins, searching for rocket parts," Mr. Field said. "Then he spends hours in the basement mixing chemicals for his rocket fuels. All day long he spends time alone. He never plays outside. He never has friends over."

"But look how happy he looks out there," said Winona.

"He seems like a born rocket scientist," said Walter.

Mr. Field's rubbed his chin, studying his son. "Uncanny," he said. "Benson is smiling. I haven't seen him smile in months."

"Sadler, I believe I know why Benson daydreams during baseball practice," said Walter. "His mind isn't on the game. His mind is on what interests him...rocketry."

"Walter gets the same way, all dreamy-like when he's writing his book," said Winona. "It's hard to get his attention."

"I'm in the writing *zone,* you might say," said Walter.

The adults watched Benson kneel next to another rocket. He was showing another Maker's Club member how to load his rocket fuel. How confident and happy he appeared.

"Hmmm, I see your point, Walter," said Sadler Field. "At the dinner table, Benson always talks about rocket designs and fuel formulas. He talks about nothing else. His mind seems to be overflowing with ideas."

"About science, not baseball," said Walter.

Mr. Field nodded. "Yep, that's what Benson's doing out there in right field during practice. He's mentally designing his next rocket. Walter, you've taken a load off my mind."

"And Cat will be here to protect him," said Winona

"Ruff! Ruff!" went Cat.

"Now why don't I start up the grill and you and Benson can join us for some spare ribs with some secret Wilson BBQ sauce."

"Don't mind if I do," said Mr. Field. "Benson is having the time of his life.

Winona eyed her husband. "I didn't know there is a secret Wilson BBQ sauce," she said.

"It's so secret I'm the only one who knows the

recipe," said Walter. "Ribs with Wilson secret sauce coming right up."

Every day the twins rose early to practice tetherball before school started. Soon Winslow became so good at stretching high on his tiptoes to bat the yellow ball, Whitney rarely returned it.

One morning recess, Winslow and Whitney stood by the tetherball circle, studying Irene. Before each game Irene, the Tetherball Queen would point to her opponent and announced how long the game would last.

"Twelve seconds," she said to a third-grade girl.

"Fifteen seconds or less," she said to a fifth- grade boy.

Between games, Winslow noticed, Irene checked the playground to make sure everyone was following her rules.

"I said only fifth-graders can use the Hula-Hoops," she screamed at a first-grader who was hula-hooping nearby.

"I said fourth-graders can only play in Fort Wilderness on Mondays," she shouted at a fourth-grader sitting on top of the climbing structure.

The twins cringed.

"Irene rules this playground with an iron fist," Winslow said.

"And she uses that iron fist to kill the tetherball," said Whitney. "The sooner you beat her, the sooner we can enjoy recess."

Winslow nodded. "I think I'm almost ready," he said. "Friday will be the challenge day."

Friday morning, Winslow got up extra early and jogged five laps around the playground.

"I'm all warmed up for the big tetherball match with Irene," he said at breakfast.

"Today's the day Winslow will dethrone, Irene, the Tetherball Queen," Whitney said.

"Good luck, dear," said Winona. "We'll be rooting for you from right here."

"Remember, my boy, it's all about timing," said Walter. "Timing is everything to win in tetherball."

"But I also have a strategy," said Winslow. "I've found Irene's weak spot."

"Weak spot? Great Scott?" said Walter. "What weak spot? The girl looks unstoppable."

"You'll have to wait until morning recess and see," said Winslow. "But when I'm playing I need Whitney to join the four-square game."

"Four-square?" said Whitney. "But I'm no good at four-square."

"It doesn't matter," said Winslow. "I just need you to join the four-square game as part of my plan."

When the morning bell rang, the twins left for school. The next time it rang it was recess time, time for the tetherball match.

Waving toward the Coots Apartment, the twins

stepped onto the playground. While Whitney took off for the four-square court, Winslow joined the line at the tetherball circle,

"First victim," Irene called out, and a tall third-grader entered the ring. Irene looked around the playground before pointing at the boy.

"I'll beat you in eight seconds, Thomas," she said.

Irene tossed up the yellow ball, rose onto her tiptoes and batted the ball hard. Around and around it went, so high Thomas was unable to touch it. Shorter and shorter the string got, until, eight seconds later, the ball tapped the pole, and the game was over.

"Next victim," Irene called out.

One after the other, Irene beat her opponents, most often with a single swat. Finally, it was Winslow's turn. With butterflies in his stomach, he stepped into the circle.

"Well, it's the new kid," Irene said. "You're about to see why I rule this playground."

Winslow squared his shoulder with the tetherball pole. He spread his feet and crouched slightly.

"Ready, Irene," he said.

"Hurrah, for Winslow!" Walter shouted from the Coots Apartment.

"Winslow! Winslow! He's our man!" cheered Winona.

Irene laughed. "So your name is Win...slow," she said. "Well, it's about to change to Lose...fast. Six seconds, Losefast."

Irene smacked the yellow ball. It twirled far over Winslow's head. On the way around, Irene swatted the ball again, sending it spinning even faster around the pole.

The string grew shorter and shorter. Winslow had to act fast. The next time the ball came around, he leaped up with his hand stretched high. *Bam!* He socked the yellow sphere, and for the first time it started in the other direction.

"Lucky hit!" said Irene, and she swatted it back to Winslow.

Bam! Winslow hit the ball back Irene and she to him. Back and forth the yellow orb went to the thrill of the other kids on the playground.

"That's the way, Winslow!" Walter called.

"Two, four, six, eight, who do we appreciate!" Winona cheered. "Winslow! Winslow!"

Meanwhile, across the asphalt, Winona stood at the four-square court. The moment she stepped into the first square to join the game, she caught Irene's eye.

"Hey, you, new kid," Irene shouted, batting the ball back to Winslow. "Who said you can play on my playground?"

Now was Winslow's chance. When he saw Irene's attention was off the game, he smacked the ball as hard as he could. It whirled over the girl's head. The other children gasped. No one had ever hit the tetherball past Irene before. Around the ball went, and Winslow hit it again.

This time, however, Irene was waiting for the ball with her arm stretched up high. But to her surprise, it didn't go above her head. It spun low near her knees and passed her.

"Hurrah!" Winona called from the Coots

Apartment.

"Timing, Winslow!" said Walter. "Get in the groove and time your moves!"

By now the tetherball string had unwound from the pole and was still going in Winslow's direction. His next hit sent it high over Irene, and the next one went low, confusing the girl completely.

The other kids cheered wildly. Winslow was winning the game. He kept the ball spinning past Irene, high, low, high, high, low.

"Go, Winslow! Go!" chanted the crowd.

Shorter and shorter grew the tetherball string. Around and around went the yellow ball. Then it tapped the pole, and Winslow had won.

"Hurrah!" everyone cheered.

Irene scowled at Winslow. For the first time in her life, she stepped out of the tetherball circle. Frowning, the dethroned queen stood at the end of the line of players and waited for her turn to come again.

10

On Saturday the Happy Valley Coots faced the Mayfield Gophers in their first baseball game. The grassy area on both sides of the Wilson's apartment was filled with parents in lounge chairs. The Wilsons had cleared off half the bench for the Coot players to sit on when they weren't in the field.

"Nice of you to invite us in," said Mr. Field.

"The Wilsons love visitors," said Winona.

"Bratwurst! Get your bratwurst here!" shouted Walter, who stood by his grill loaded with sausages. By his side stood Dan, the Can Man, handing out cans of soda from an ice chest.

"Please recycle the cans," he said. "Please return

them to me."

Cathy and Gavin arrived pushing Rose in a stroller. The baby wore a black and white Coot baseball cap.

"Gavin! Cathy!" said Walter. "How have you been?"

"Busy, that's for sure," said Gavin. "I'm doing my student teaching and that sure keeps me busy. And having a baby sure is busy work."

Cathy handed Winona a bouquet of daffodils. "These are for making your Coots Apartment even brighter," she said.

Miss Potts arrived waving a French flag. She wore her blue beret, and a T-shirt with I ♥ PARIS on the front.

"I watched the most wonderful French movie on TV last night," she told the Wilsons. "It was all in French with subtitles."

"Ooo la laa," said Walter.

Kelly, the Maker Club leader, showed up wearing his backpack full of bricks.

"I see, you're still carrying that load on your shoulders, young man," said Walter.

"I leave next week on my thru-hike of the Pacific Coast Trail," Kelly said. "When I tried on my backpack with the regular hiking gear inside, it felt as light as a feather."

"Play ball!" shouted the umpire.

"Coots! Coots!" the people around the Coots Apartment cheered.

Being the home team, the Coot players ran out to the field. Whitney played third base and Winslow first. Nora was on the mound, and Benson stood in right field, gazing at the sky. With only eight players on the team, center field remained empty.

"Batter up!" shouted the umpire and the first Gopher player came to the plate.

Nora pitched a fastball, and the batter hit a grounder past Lilly Spring at second base. At once Cat leaped from the Coots Apartment and took off after it. The Gopher batter raced for first base, but before he got there, the dog had grabbed the ball and run to

Winslow. With one foot on the bag, Winslow took the ball from Cat's mouth.

"Um, you're out, I think," said the umpire.

"Bravo, Cat," said Walter.

"Uncanny, that dog," said Mr. Field.

A roar of protest rose from the Gopher players and coach.

The umpire shrugged. "I read the entire Little League rulebook last night," he said. "It said nothing about dogs on the field."

"*Ruff! Ruff!*" went Cat.

"In that case, I think we have our ninth player," Sadler Field said. "Cat can play center field."

"Excellent idea," said Walter. He padded the dog on the snout. "Go to it, boy. Win one for the Coots."

"*Ruff! Ruff!*" went Cat and he raced into center field and sat there.

"Play ball," said the umpire.

The game continued. But even with Cat in the field, the Gophers scored ten runs in the first inning. When the Coots came to bat they went out one-two-three. In the second inning, the Gophers scored ten more runs. They would have scored even more if Cat hadn't made a brilliant running catch for the third out.

"Uncanny, that dog," said Mr. Field.

The Coots, however, again failed to score. They did no better in the third and fourth inning. By the end of the fifth inning the score was 50 to 0.

"OK, that's enough," Mr. Field called out. He walked up to the Gopher manager and shook his hand. "Your team is just too much for us," he said. "We concede. The game is yours."

"Then I invite everyone over to the Coots Apartment for bratwursts," Walter called out. "Come and get it."

Despite the Coots' lose, the afternoon turned out happy for everyone. Cathy found new customers for her flower business; the twins made new friends; Dan collected enough cans for his daily quota, and Benson announced, "I had lots of time to think in right field. I can't wait to begin mixing my new rocket fuel."

The star of the evening, however, was Cat.

Everyone made sure to give him the end piece of bratwurst as a reward for being such a good ball player.

"Ruff! Ruff!"

As evening came on, many people remained by the Coots Apartment, chatting and laughing. Two guests, in particular, caught Winona's interest.

"Walter, look over by the swing set," she said.

Walter rolled a few sausages on the grill and looked toward the asphalt. Miss Potts and Mr. Field sat side by side on the swings. They held hands and they swung gently back and forth.

"Ooo la laaa," said Walter. "I think Miss Potts might have found a partner to go with her to Paris."

11

One evening in May, Happy Valley Elementary School held its annual Open House. All day the students cleaned their classrooms, straightened out their desks, and put up writing assignments on the bulletin boards for their parents to admire.

After a pizza dinner in the Coots Apartment, the Wilsons walked over to the school building. Walter brought his new video camera to record the event. He walked down the hallway with the camera held against his eyeball.

"I don't want to miss a single moment of this excellent evening," he said.

"There's a painting I did in art class," said Whitney, pointing to a picture on a hallway bulletin board.

"A masterpiece," said Winona.

"Only the best," said Walter, aiming his camera.

"And there's my drawing," said Winslow. "But the art teacher hung it upside down.

"No problem," said Walter. He turned his video camera around. "Now it will appear the way you intended.

The Wilsons entered the fourth-grade classroom. The place bustled with students showing their parents schoolwork and school projects. Nora Lee stood at a computer with her parents viewing a PowerPoint presentation she made on Africa, while Benson Field was by the science table demonstrating to Mr. Field a robot he built with Legos.

Miss Potts stood by her desk, chatting with parents. Winona couldn't help noticing that Mr. Field kept glancing at her.

Meanwhile, Walter wandered about the room,

recording all the activity. He pointed his camera at the narrow room in the back of the classroom.

"And there's the tidy, tiny room we stayed in our first night in Happy Valley," he said. "Excellent accommodations but for that nasty bell on the wall."

"Voila! Good evening, parents and students," Miss Potts called from the front of the room. "Welcome to our Open House. The boys and girls have worked very hard this year. I hope you enjoy all the schoolwork on the walls and desks. Help yourselves to a French pastry our room parents have brought us. Merci."

"Ooo la laaaaaa," said Walter, as he grabbed a croissant off the back table.

Next, the voice of Mrs. Franklin, the school principal, came over the intercom. "Greetings, students, parents, and friends. In a half-hour, please proceed to the gym for an important announcement by the Happy Valley School Board."

After Winslow and Whitney showed Walter and Winona the stories they wrote, the clay pots they made, and the A grades on the math tests they took, the Wilsons walked down the hall to the school gym. Although the rows of folding chairs were nearly filled, the room was surprisingly silent.

The Wilsons sat next to Nora Lee and her parents.

"Great Scott," Walter said to Mr. Lee. "Everyone's so glum."

"I thought an Open House was a happy occasion," said Winona.

"Not this one," said Mr. Lee. "We believe the School Board is about to announce something the parents have feared for a long time. Prepare for sad news, Wilsons."

Walter pointed his video camera at six people sitting on the gym stage. A white-haired man wearing a white suit stood and walked to a podium.

"Good evening," he said into a microphone. "I'm Taylor Tate owner of Tate Realtors, Tate Auto Body, and Tate Taco Shop here in Happy Valley. I'm also president of the Happy Valley School Board." He paused for some applause but received none. He continued in a low tone, "Now, as most of you know, school enrollment is way down in our town and your school board has had to make a tough decision. Tonight it's sad for me to announce that due to a decrease in school tax funds, we must close Happy Valley Elementary School. This fall, students in Happy Valley will attend other schools in the district.

A groan rose from the crowd.

"But our kids have been going to this school since kindergarten," a woman called out.

"The reason we moved to Happy Valley is to attend this school," shouted a man.

"I'm sorry, but our decision is final," said Taylor Tate. "Meeting adjourned. Eat at Tate Taco Shop tonight and receive a complimentary dessert with your meal."

The Wilsons left the school saddened.

"So much for our one and only Happy Valley Open House," said Winslow.

"Just when I found a place I like, it closes," said Whitney.

"I'll miss the sound of children playing during the day while I draw," said Winona.

Walter held up his video camera and viewed the videos he had taken during the Open House. "I'll even miss that bell," he said.

12

The last day of school in early June was Field Day. During the afternoon, after cleaning out their desks, the students took part in games and races on the baseball field. The fourth-graders began with a sack race, which Nora Lee won. Next came an egg and spoon race where victory went to Whitney. Aft that was a water balloon toss during which Benson got soaked, and a three-legged race that Whitney and Winslow won together. At the end, everyone got a prize, a cherry Popsicle, for participation.

At 3:00 the fourth-graders said good-bye to Miss Potts and left for home.

"Farewell fourth grade," said Winona back in the Coots Apartment.

"So Happy Valley Elementary School forever," said Winslow.

The first weeks of summer offered the Wilsons warm days and moonlit nights. The family whiled away the hours writing, reading, and playing pick-up-sticks in the long apartment. During the afternoon when the automatic lawn sprinklers went off in the baseball field, the twins put on their swimsuits and leaped back and forth in the stiff, pulsating water jets. Often Nora Lee, Benson Field, and Cat joined them.

One afternoon Walter closed his laptop lid and announced, "Period. The end. I've finished the first draft of *The Up and Downs of the Elevator Family*."

"Congratulations, Walter," said Winona. "And I've finished my final sketch. It shows us staying in that wonderful room in front of Harrods Department Store in London, England. Weren't those giant windows grand?"

"Only the best," said Walter. "What a happy

Christmas that was."

"Walter, I think Happy Valley is the nicest place we've ever stayed in," said Winona. "Must we move again?"

"I'm afraid the school board was clear," said Walter. "When Happy Valley Elementary School closes, the playground will close as well. That includes our Coots Apartment."

Winona looked out at Whitney, Winslow, and Cat playing in the sprinklers. "But the twins have never been happier," she said. "And they've made wonderful friends here."

"Don't worry, Winona," said Walter. "One thing I was reminded from writing this book about our family is that things always work out for the best."

On July 4 Happy Valley held its annual 4th of July parade. The parade started in the school parking lot. The twins, wearing their baseball uniforms, marched with the Coots Little League team. Cat, wearing a black baseball cap, marched with them.

Winona had decorated the Coots Apartment with

red, white, and blue bunting. She and Walter cheered as the parade left the school parking lot. In the lead was a red fire truck with its red light flashing. The parade grand marshal, Taylor Tate, stood in back waving at the crowd and handing out discount coupons to Tate Auto Body.

"Oh, Walter isn't this exciting," said Winona.

"Look, Cathy is driving her van in the parade," said Walter. "And it's all decorated with red, white, and blue flowers."

"And there's Gavin dressed up a Uncle Sam," said Winona. "He's pushing baby Rose in a stroller."

After the parade, workmen showed up of the baseball field with crates of tubes and wires, the equipment to set off the evening fireworks. To the Wilsons' delight, the Happy Valley firework display would be shot off right outside the Coots Apartment. They invited all their Happy Valley friends—the Lees, the Field, Miss Potts, Cathy, Gavin, Rose, and Dan, the Can Man—for a picnic barbecue before the show.

Around seven the guest started to arrive. "It's an

all American barbecue," said Walter, who stood at the grill wearing a Kiss the Cook apron. "Hot dogs, potatoes chips, and ice cream. *Hot diggity dog. We're having hot dogs*."

"*Ruff! Ruff!*" went Cat.

While the grown-up chatted and drank lemonade, the kid ran around the field squirting each other with squirt guns. The evening was warm, so no one minded getting wet.

Near nightfall, families arrived on the field and spread blankets on the grass.

"It's the first time we've ever watched fireworks right from our own home," said Winona.

The first firework went off—*Boom*!—and everyone cheered.

"A *blue peony*," Winslow announced.

The second firework cracked the sky.

"And that was a *yellow willow*," said Winslow.

"Winslow, since when are you such a firework expert," Whitney asked.

"I've been studying types of fireworks on the

Internet," said Winslow. "There's an *orange beehive* and another *peony*."

"Excellent," said Walter. "Similar to identifying birds."

"Remember the time we stayed in that tiny lone cabin far out in a field," said Winona.

"Yes, I wrote about that in my book," said Walter. "The cabin was owned by the Hudson Firework Company. It was where they mixed the chemicals for the fireworks."

"I had wondered why the cabin was all alone far out in a field," said Winona.

"How lucky we were not to have lit a candy that evening," said Whitney.

Throughout the firework display, Winslow continued to call out names. "That's a *spinner*. There are a *brocade* and two *comets*. That was a *palm*, and there's my favorite, a *school of fish*."

The show ended with the usual loud and bright barrage of booms, bangs, and flashes. Afterward, Sadler Field stood in front of the crowd to make an announcement. "Ladies and gentlemen, we have an extra finale to our firework show tonight. My son, Benson, has made a very special firework for us all."

At this point, Benson walked up to a large tube stuck in the ground. He wore a new T-shirt his father had bought him during a visit to the Jet Propulsion Laboratory in Pasadena. On the front it said, YES, I *AM* A ROCKET SCIENTIST.

"Hurrah, for Benson," the Wilsons cheered from the Coots Apartment.

Benson bowed and began the countdown. The crowd joined him.

"Ten…nine…eight…seven…six…five…four…three …two…one…*Blast off!"*

A loud swoosh came from the tube and a white streak of sparkles shot upward. Moments later, a huge bouquet of sparkles burst in the sky. It was the best firework of the evening.

"Fantabulous," said Winslow. That was a willow, a pistil, spinner, and three comets all in one."

"Bravo, Benson," Walter called out. "That boy has

talent."

The next evening Irene Towne and her mother, Angela, visited the Coots Apartment. Ever since her defeat as Tetherball Queen, Irene had been friendly with the twins. She now ran out to the field with them to catch fireflies. The bug's blinking lights dipping about the field matched the twinkling lights strung along the roof of the Coots Apartment.

Walter, Winona, and Angela Towne sat in lounge chairs by the long apartment drinking iced tea.

"Walter and Winona, as you know I'm president of the Happy Valley Elementary School PTA," Angela said. "The parents are arranging a fundraiser to try and save our school."

"Excellent," said Walter. "My book should be ready by then, and I'll donate all proceeds to the Save Our School Fund."

"And I'll make some of our famous Wilson chocolate chip cookies to sell," said Winona.

Angela Lee took a sip of iced tea. "Yes, every little bit will help," she said.

"How much money do we need to keep the school open in the fall?" Winona asked.

The woman looked toward the school and shook her head. "A lot," she said. "Taylor Tate says we'll need to raise at least two million dollars."

"Great Scott," said Walter. "That's a lot of cookie dough."

"Who in Happy Valley has that kind of money?" said Winona. "We need a wealthy donor."

"Yes, a benefactor who sees the value of education would be a godsend," Angela Lee.

Walter went silent. He stroked his chin.

Winona knew that look. Walter was thinking up a plan. When Walter smiled, she smiled, too. Had her husband thought up a way to save the school?

Meanwhile, the twins and Irene ran around the field catching lightning bugs. The sun had set and the air had cooled.

"What a lovely time of the day," said Angela Lee.

"The Purple Time," said Winona.

13

The Save Our School Fundraiser took place on the last Saturday of July. The PTA set up booths around the baseball diamond, and in each booth a parent or teacher sold sometime to raise money. In one booth Cathy and Gavin sold flowers. In another Mrs. Lee sold raffle ticket. Miss Potts sat in another booth selling T-shirts that read I ♥ Paris on the front, and Sadler Field sat in the next booth selling T-shirts that read **Go Coots.**

Kelly took a break from his Pacific Crest Trail thru-hike to sell hiking sticks and photos in another booth.

"I've hiked one-thousand miles so far," he told the Wilsons. "I only have one-thousand, six hundred and fifty miles to go."

By second base, Walter, Winona, Whitney, and Winslow sat in a booth with a pile of *The Ups and Downs of the Elevator Family* on a card table.

"Step on up, and read all about us," Walter called out. "The Elevator Family. Read about our adventures when we stayed in the Otis room at the San Francisco Hotel, in the Toll 2 cabin on a bridge over the Mississippi River, and in a little cabin with a great view high up on a tower in the North Woods of Minnesota. Only the best! Only the best will do for this family. All book sale proceeds go to the Save Our School Fund."

All morning people lined up in front of his Walter's booth to buy a book. With a black Sharpie pen Walter, Winona, Whitney, and Winslow signed each one.

In the meantime, Taylor Tate stood on a stage by home plate. Beside him stood a large cardboard thermometer. At the top it read:

$2,000,000
OUR SCHOOL SAVED

As the PTA made money from the fair, the school board president, using a red felt marker, colored in the amount on the thermometer.

"Four thousand dollars raised," he announced around ten o'clock. Then he colored in a tiny amount at the bottom of the thermometer. "Need to sell your house? Call Tate Realtor."

"Six thousand dollar," he said at noon, and he colored in another small space. "Have lunch at Tate Bistro and enjoy our Save Our School special."

Winslow looked at the thermometer on the stage and frowned. "We'll need to sell another million books to reach our goal," he said.

"Time is running out to save our school," said Whitney. "In two hours the fundraiser closes and then it's bye-bye Happy Valley Elementary."

Walter wiped his brow with his handkerchief. "Home sweat home," he said. "Excuse me, but I have to go meet someone."

Winona smiled inwardly. "Certainly, dear," she said.

Walter grabbed his car keys off the card table and walked toward the parking lot.

"Where's dad going?" asked Whitney.

"He looked like he had something up his sleeve," said Winslow.

"Yes, I think he has a plan," said Winona. "And you know your father's plans are always good ones."

In the next hour, the red thermometer mark rose only an inch.

"Seven thousand dollars," said Taylor Tate. "Have a dent in your fender? Get it repaired at Tate Auto Body. Two fenders for the price of one special, during the Save Our School Fundraiser."

Another hour passed. Winona, Whitney, and Winslow were about to close the book booth when they looked toward the stage. Walter stood there, whispering something into Taylor Tate's ear. The head of the school board raised his arms and let out a whoop. He turned to the thermometer and filled it in with the red marker all the way up to the $2,000,000 mark

"We did it," he announced. "Happy Valley School is saved!"

The crowd of parents and students across the ball field let out a cheer.

Inside the book booth Winona, Whitney, and Winslow exchanged looks.

"What just happened?" asked Whitney.

"*How* did it happen?" asked Winslow.

Winona shrugged. "I don't know what or how, but I know Walter did it again!"

At that moment, Miss Potts in the next booth cried out, "*Regardez!* A French poodle!"

The three Wilsons glanced toward the Coots Apartment. On the top step, a French poodle stood nose to nose with Cat.

"*Ruff! Ruff!*" went Cat.

"*Yap! Yap! Yap!*" went the poodle

"I know that dog," said Whitney.

"It's Oui-Oui!" said Winslow.

"Oui-Oui!" said Winona.

"Oui-Oui?" said Mrs. Potts. "I don't understand."

"Oui-Oui is Mrs. Goldengate's dog," said Winona. "We met her and her dog when we stayed in the Otis Room at the San Francisco Hotel. You don't suppose....?"

"Yes! Look in the parking lot," said Whitney.

Parked in the lot was a long, white limousine. The driver had opened the back door, and an elderly woman dressed in white Capri pants, a floral-printed shirt, and a large straw hat stepped out. It was none other than Abigail Goldengate, herself.

"Mrs. Goldengate!" Winona, Whitney, and Winslow called out.

"The Wilsons! The Elevator Family!" the woman replied. Walter walked up to the woman and escorted her to the Coots Apartment where the other Wilsons greeted her. There followed many hugs handshakes, and fist pumps.

"Gracious, Abigail," said Winona. "When we saw you last you were leaving for Montana to be with your daughter."

'That I did," said the woman. "And the past years have been the most relaxing, peaceful ones since my dear husband Gordon Goldengate passed away."

"Now you're in Happy Valley," said Whitney.

Mrs. Goldengate nudged Walter with her elbow. "Walter called me up and said your school needed help," she said.

"So she made a generous contribution to the Save Our School Fund," said Walter.

"Then I rushed here with Oui-Oui on my private jet to see you all," said Mrs. Goldengate.

"Now we won't have to leave Happy Valley," said Winona.

"And we can go to fifth grade at this school," said Winslow.

"And we can continue playing on this playground," said Whitney

"Now I can go to Paris knowing I have a job," said Mrs. Potts from her booth.

"And I'm going with her," said Sadler Field from his booth.

Gavin and Cathy walked by pushing Rose in her stroller.

"And there are two old friends from the San Francisco Hotel where I lived in the penthouse," said Mrs. Goldengate.

"Hello, Mrs. Goldengate," said Gavin. "I'm sure glad you showed up. Now I can begin my teaching career right here at Happy Valley Elementary School."

Because, guess what?" said Cathy. "Mrs. Franklin has offered Gavin the fifth-grade job."

"And we can all be together in this excellent town," said Walter.

Abigail Goldengate looked into the Coots Apartment. "And now Oui-Oui has made a new friend."

"*Ruff! Ruff!*" went Cat.

"*Yap! Yap! Yap!* " went Oui-Oui.

***B**riiiiing!*

Walter sat up in the pitch dark and scratched his belly.

"That bell," he groaned. "I forgot all about it."

"Isn't it a lovely sound?" said Winona, lying beside her husband. "The start of a new school year at Happy Valley Elementary School."

Walter reached up and pulled the light switch chord. The light lit up a long narrow room, a copy of the one in which the Wilsons had stayed their first night in Happy Valley.

Winslow and Whitney, dressed in school clothes,

stood by the door at the end of the room.

"We should be going," said Winslow.

"We don't want to be late for our first day of fifth grade," said Whitney.

"This is indeed a big day for the Wilsons," said Walter. "Not only are the twins starting school again, but after school we're moving into our new home."

Whitney opened the door and the narrow room filled with the chatter of children. After the twins left, Walter and Winona stuffed their sleeping bags in their wheeled luggage and also departed. As they stepped across the rear of the classroom, they gave the thumbs up sign to Gavin, the new fifth-grade teacher, who sat nervously behind the teacher's desk. On the desk was a vase filled with carnations. He smiled at Walter and Winona and returned their wave.

In the hallway Walter and Winona spotted the new school custodian, Dan, the Can Man, mopping a spill.

"Morning, Dan," said Walter. "How's the new job going?"

"So far, so good," the man said. "I enjoy being with the children."

"We were surprised when you took the job," said Winona. "We remember your story about the fisherman."

The man smiled. "Yes, Wilsons, but I figured a little extra money saved for a rainy day can't be too harmful."

In the school parking lot, Walter and Winona found Cathy, Rose, and Cat waiting for them. All morning they helped Cathy deliver flowers around Happy Valley. At three o'clock they picked up the twins from school and drove to their new home. The house, which was tiny, took only a month to build. It was no bigger than a one-car garage.

Taylor Tate stood on the small front porch. He handed Walter the keys to the front door. "There you go, Walter," he said. "Welcome to your new home."

"Only the best," said Walter.

"But with all the money you've made from your new book, I still don't know why you didn't build yourself a mansion," said Taylor Tate.

"This house is just what we wanted," said Walter.

"Cozy and tidy," said Winona.

"Small and compact," said Winslow.

"We're a tight-knit family," said Whitney.

The four Wilsons entered the house. They stood in the eight-foot by seven-foot living room. Although small it still had room for a sofa, two easy chairs, and a coffee table. In the back was the bathroom and kitchen. A ladder led to a loft with four feather beds.

"Fantabulous," said Winslow.

"It's ideal," said Whitney.

"Oh, Walter, it's what we've always dreamed of," said Winona.

"Only the best," said Walter. "And in the backyard, there's a barbecue pit, so we can have visitors over for picnics."

"And there's a doghouse for Cat," said Winona.

"*Ruff! Ruff!*" went the dog.

The next thing Walter did was to open his wheeled luggage and take out the Home Sweat Home sampler. With great ceremony, he hung it on the wall above the small fireplace.

"Home Sweat Home hangs wherever the Wilsons stay," he said.

"And it has hung in many wonderful places," said Winona.

"But I hope it will hang in this Happy Valley house for a long time," said Whitney.

"At least until we go off to college," said Winslow.

"Hear, hear," said Wilsons said together.

"*Ruff! Ruff*"*!* went Cat.

For the longest time, the four Wilsons stood in the middle of room admiring their new home.

Finally, Winslow broke the silence. He held up a cardboard tube and said, "Anyone for a game of pick up sticks?"

Made in the USA
San Bernardino, CA
27 April 2020